CARDINALS
APPEAR WHEN
ANGELS
ARE NEAR

A story about how one child deals with the loss and grief of losing loved ones.

Cindy Biggins-Joseph

ISBN 978-1-64559-323-2 (Paperback)
ISBN 978-1-64559-324-9 (Hardcover)
ISBN 978-1-64559-325-6 (Digital)

Copyright © 2020 Cindy Biggins-Joseph
All rights reserved
First Edition

All rights reserved. No part of this publication may be reproduced, distributed, or transmitted in any form or by any means, including photocopying, recording, or other electronic or mechanical methods without the prior written permission of the publisher. For permission requests, solicit the publisher via the address below.

Covenant Books, Inc.
11661 Hwy 707
Murrells Inlet, SC 29576
www.covenantbooks.com

This book is dedicated to my beautiful Mother and friend Mrs. Ella Mae Green-Biggins who passed away on September 15, 2019. You are missed every day.

Right now Mom is flying with all of her Cardinal friends, traveling around to make sure everything is alright with our families. I love you Ella Mae and always will.

Forever in Love Cindy.

Also in my heart,

Annie Lee Johnson aka "Lee Lee" (Godmother)
Nathaniel Biggins aka "PaPa" (Dad #1)
Woodrow Wilson aka "Woody" (Dad #2)

I hope y'all are looking down on me and saying, "We did a good job with her."

With a life span of fifteen years, the cardinal holds a symbol of hope to the hopeless, joy to the joyless, and rebirth to the saddened.

If you are lucky enough to see a *red bird*, ask yourself, who has come back to make sure that I'm alright?

Whenever you're struggling with life—whether it be addiction, the loss of a loved one, your family dynamics, school issues, or whatever—just know that tomorrow is another day to make things right. Look for help in those that are willing to help you.

It might not be a *red bird*; it could be a teacher, your pastor, a nurse, or your neighbor.

You may never know at that moment who's trying to let you know that you are loved, and life definitely goes on; however, when the time is right in your heart, you will know who it is.

Cardinals Appear When Angels Are Near is about the love between a grandparent and a grandchild.

When I, Darnell, a.k.a. "DJ," was born, my mother was seventeen years old. We lived with her parents, and I was loved from the moment my mother conceived me. My grandparents adored me, especially my granddad, PaPa.

PaPa was the kind of man who sought the good in everything. He was a churchgoing man who believed that anyone who lived in his home had to attend church, even when you didn't want to. But I always wanted to go.

PaPa was a loving and kind man. His wife of sixty-three years grew to know that whatever PaPa said had a meaning, and he always turned out right for our family.

Before I was born, my mother got married to my dad in Waxahachie, Texas, without my grandparents' permission. Then my dad left for the Army. Shortly after, my Mom got the news from a visit of some military men that my dad had been killed in action. He died a hero, saving his troops from an enemy ambush. I look at his military medals all of the time. My grandparents stepped up, especially my PaPa, and the rest is history.

As I grew, PaPa was there every step of the way. He became my dad since my own dad was killed in the Army. My Mom keeps a picture of my dad in every room. I would have loved to know him, but if he was half the man my PaPa is, then my Mom did great!

Our home was warm and loving, and my grandparents encouraged and supported my Mom in completing her education. She excelled at Texas Southern University and Thurgood Marshall Law School and became the first African American female district attorney in our small community of Ennis, Texas.

Mom kept long hours, and we continued to live with my grandparents since Mom felt I would always have someone looking after me. I knew how hard she was working to try to be both Mom and Dad to me. But what she didn't realize was I had a dad—PaPa!

One day, as we were leaving my little league baseball practice, we saw a red bird. PaPa told me a story. He said, "If anyone is ever lucky enough to see a red bird, then hear a red bird sing, then that person is very special and has an angel looking over them all his or her life."

All I could say was, "Wow!" If PaPa says it, then it must be true.

When I got home, I told my mother what PaPa had said. Mom told me, "Ah, that's good, it's just your father looking to see how you are doing and how proud he is of you. I saw that red bird yesterday and told him you were turning out to be a fine young man, and PaPa was doing an excellent job helping to raise you." Mom kissed me and started cooking again.

After that, I never saw a red bird again, although I looked for one for about a year but with no such luck.

My PaPa is such an amazing man. He knows everything. I'm learning a lot, we go fishing, he taught me how to do calculus, how to excel in school, and he told me, "If you can't be smart, be quiet and let other students learn." We even talk about girls; you know, the kind of stuff a young African American male needs to know. Like "No means no," what it's like to have a first kiss, and how I will be in "*like*" many times but "*love*" only once, like PaPa and my Big Mama.

We would have the best long walks and talks, and at the end of them, PaPa would always say, "Hey, DJ, I love you."

And I would say, "Hey, PaPa, I love you back."

My middle school years were awesome, and it was like someone or something was guiding me. I didn't think my life could get any better than this. All along the way, my PaPa was right there.

One day, when I walked in the house, my Mom was there early. I ran to hug her and said, "You're home early, you must have won a major case today."

My Mom looked at me and said, "No, Big Mama is very sick."

I was baffled, because she was the rock of our home. My Big Mama was a quiet woman, but she could give you a look that said everything. I never knew her to be sick. Mom said, "She has breast cancer, and it's in its last stage."

I said, "Why didn't anyone tell me?" When I went into my grandparents' room, PaPa was sitting beside their bed, reading the Bible to her. They were holding hands, smiling lovingly at each other. They were talking, remembering their earlier days, and laughing occasionally. As the days went by, my Mom and PaPa tried to make it as normal for me as possible. Every day, when I returned from school, PaPa would be swinging on the porch swing where he and Big Mama would swing and talk, holding hands for hours. I would always hug and kiss him and rush upstairs to see Big Mama and share my day with her.

One day, as I was rushing home, I heard a sound that I hadn't heard in years. There was a red cardinal singing in the big tree outside my grandparents' window. I looked up, I stood there for a minute thinking, *Man, how sweet is that?* I rushed up stairs to their room, just in time to see that same red bird fly off the window ledge that Big Mama and PaPa loved to keep open.

As I rushed in, PaPa and my Mom were crying as Big Mama lay there, peacefully asleep. I knew.

The funeral was pleasant and huge. Big Mama would have said, "First class all the way." I miss her terribly.

After that, life slowly resumed but was really never the same. PaPa finally slowed down, and Mom was at home a lot more. PaPa and I still did everything together, just slower. Now I was in high school, excelling in everything, grades were excellent. I was in all sports as though there was something extra helping me along.

Every now and then, I would see PaPa smiling and talking to someone, swinging on the porch swing just like he used to do with Big Mama. PaPa was my rock. I admired and loved him and told him so often.

Wow! Seventeen came fast for me. Almost a senior, that summer before my eighteenth birthday and right before my senior year, I could not have been in a better spot in my life. At eighteen, you think the world is at your grasp; at least, that's what PaPa tells me.

At home, he was always reading his Bible, telling me stories of when he and Big Mama were young, how they met on a train ride from Ennis, Texas, to Dallas, Texas, going to the state fair, how Big Mama ignored him all day as he trailed her all around the fair, asking her name until she just could not take it anymore and said, "Ella Mae." He told me how they fell in love on that train ride back to Ennis—she was fifteen, and he was seventeen—and how at seventeen, they got married at the courthouse in Waxahachie, Texas. I love that story.

One day, I came home from school. Mom was cooking in the kitchen and said PaPa was upstairs resting.

"Resting? He never rests. He must have had a long day at the church. I need to tell him about my graduation plans."

Mom said, "Don't tire him out. You know how much y'all love to talk."

As I began to tell him, he just smiled and said, "Man, you're going to knock all the girls' socks off." The window was up, and a cool breeze was flowing in. PaPa fell asleep, and I left the room.

Weeks went by, and resting for PaPa seemed to be everyday now. I became used to it. Sometimes we would talk, but most of the time, he was asleep. I'd just sit there until he woke up.

On this particular day, the sun was shining, the wind was breezy, no clouds in the sky; and I was happy! I ran home to give PaPa some great news. I finally got up the nerve to ask the prettiest girl at school to prom, and she said yes! I couldn't wait to tell him; after all, we practiced for months on how I was going to ask her.

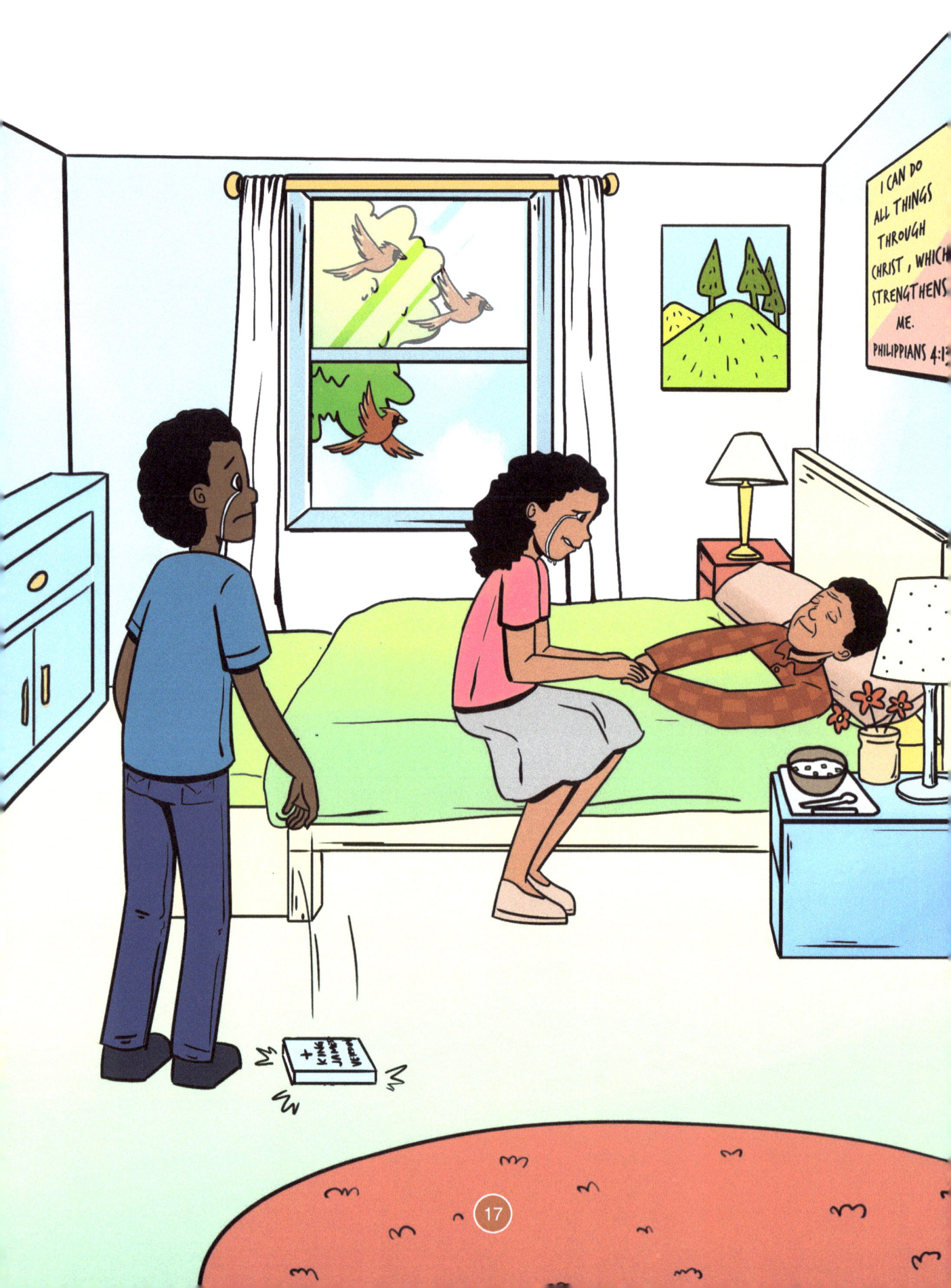

When I reached the bedroom door, I saw my Mom sitting next to the bed, holding PaPa's hand, and singing to him. My heart sank. It reminded me of Big Mama. My Mom said, "He's okay, just sleeping."

As she was saying that, PaPa woke up and said, "Open the window, I want to feel the breeze."

Mom opened the window, and PaPa saw me. He asked me to come over. I told him the great news about prom, and he said, "She would be crazy not to go with you. After all, you're my grandson, aren't you?" And we laughed.

Mom came back in with the dinner she had made for him. PaPa asked me to go downstairs and get his Bible. There was something he wanted me to read. Then he said, "Hey, DJ, I love you, son."

I smiled and went downstairs to get the Bible, then the phone rang. I told the caller, "My Mom is upstairs with my PaPa, can I take a message?"

When I reach the bedroom door, to my amazement, I saw three red birds fly away from the window ledge. I yelled, "Mom, did you see that?"

My Mom turned to me and said, "PaPa is gone to heaven to be with Big Mama."

My heart dropped as I dropped the Bible. I ran to the bed. I cried for hours at his bedside until he was carried away. I told my mother, "Another funeral, first class all the way."

My senior year came and went. I didn't even go to prom; nothing particularly exciting. I would sit on the porch swing for hours every day, thinking about my Big Mama and PaPa. Summer turned into fall. My Mom started working more and more.

I got accepted to Texas Southern University in Houston, Texas; far enough but not too far from my memories. Those college years were up and down. It seemed like nothing was going right for me since PaPa passed away. I would try to talk to Mom, but she always had interruptions at work. She had gotten more and more promotions at her job as though she was working to ease the pain of losing both Big Mama and PaPa, and me being away at college.

College became more and more tedious. I lost interest, I had no one to share my thoughts or to talk with. I was very depressed. I was just going through the motions, because it's what my Mom and grandparents wanted me to do. I had no real interest in college. I managed to squeak by each year.

One day as I was walking to class, I saw this girl. She was the most beautiful girl I'd ever seen. I remember PaPa saying, "You'd be in '*like*' a lot but in '*love*' only once."

I followed her to her class. I looked in her class door window and tapped the window to get her attention. She looked back at me like I was crazy and turned her head. Luckily our classes were in the same building. But when I got out of my class she was gone.

I didn't know what to do, I don't even know her name. Did she live on campus? Off campus? I had never seen her before on campus and didn't know where to look. I just knew she was beautiful!

I looked all over the building, on campus and in the library, but with no luck. I knew I had lost her until next week's class. I needed to find her now. I wasn't giving up.

A week went by, and I ran to that class where I saw her the first time. She was not there. All that day, I was totally sad. The next couple of days went by, and nothing—I mean nothing—seemed to be going right for me. I failed a class. Summer school looked to be in my future. I was struggling really bad. I couldn't preregister for any of my classes, Mom was in court all of the time. Man, I wished PaPa was here right now; he would know or say something on how to get back on track.

I went back to my dorm room and, for some reason, thought about and got out that Bible my PaPa had asked me to get before he passed away. As I opened it, a letter fell out. It was addressed to "My Best Friend DJ." I had not opened that Bible since the day my PaPa passed.

When I read it, he told me of how proud he was of me, how I brought him much happiness and joy. PaPa wrote, "It was an honor being your PaPa." He would always be with me, no matter where I was and what I was doing. He told me to be strong and that I would be able to talk to him any time, any place, or any day, no matter what. There was a scripture attached, and it read, "Yea, though I walk through the valley of the shadows of death, I will fear no evil for thou art with me" (Psalm 23).

The last thing he wrote was:

> Hey, DJ, I love you.
> Signed, PaPa, Always.

I never got to tell him I loved him back that day he died. Tears fell from my eyes and slid down my cheeks, and suddenly, it seemed as though a cool breeze came over me. I stopped crying and went outside to sit in the courtyard under the big beautiful trees. As I was in deep thought, I heard a familiar sound singing in the trees. When I looked up, there were three *red birds,* and they didn't fly away. They continued to sing as I had this great conversation with my PaPa, Big Mama, and Dad. I remembered my PaPa saying, "When cardinals appear, angels are near."

Right then and there, I knew it was *my family* watching over me—the three of them—telling me things were going to be all right, (and the grieving over them should stop, they are happy), and then I said, "Hey, I love y'all back."

The next afternoon, I went into the dining hall. To my amazement, there she was. I tapped her on her shoulder and said, "Hi, my name is Darnell. DJ for short. What's yours?"

She looked at me and said, "Kaye. Nice to meet you." From that point on, we were inseparable.

I called Mom weekly and told her about Kaye and how happy we are. My grades had improved, I was on the Dean's list, and Kaye and I would graduate from law school next week. I told my mother, "I wish PaPa was here to know that I found 'The One.'"

Mom said, "He knows. I'm looking at a red bird out our window now and I told him. He knows, baby, he knows."

I told my Mom that grief is an emotion that's hard to escape. No matter how hard I tried to get over PaPa and Big Mama's death, I just couldn't stop feeling sad until I read PaPa's letter. It was like he knew I was going to have a really hard time getting over his death. PaPa's words eased my heart and calmed me down.

Now that Kaye and I are married, we both are successful attorneys and have three beautiful children of our own—Chamelle, Darnell, and Michelle. I never stop telling them stories of my dad, Big Mama, and PaPa, and the angels who watch over and guide us as red birds.

ABOUT THE AUTHOR

Cindy Biggins-Joseph, author of *I Want My Brother Back*, is a retired assistant principal of twenty-two years with a total of thirty years in education from Houston, Texas. She is the mother of three and the grandmother of five.

While growing up in Fort Worth and Ennis, Texas, she fondly remembers stories told to her by her parents of how her mother, Ella Mae, and her dad, Nathaniel Biggins, met. One morning, she looked out her bedroom door and saw a beautiful red bird singing in her backyard tree. Her thoughts immediately went to her godmother, Annie Lee Johnson, and her two dads, Nathaniel Biggins and Woodrow Wilson, who are now deceased.

Wow! It's going to be a great day, she thought, *because my angel is looking after me.*

Her second book, *Cardinals Appear When Angels Are Near*, follows the life of DJ from birth to growing up in a loving household, his struggles when he loses his loved ones, his depression in his college years, to his rebirth of knowing his family will always be there to guide him no matter what.

Cardinals Appear When Angels Are Near shows the binding love that can never be broken between a grandchild with his grandparents—especially his granddad—even after heaven receives them.

Talkspace Grief Counseling

- Grief Poems: Comforting Words To Help With Grief and Loss
    - familyfriendlypoems.com
- View Grief And Loss For Children
    - s.healthnwell.com/mentalhealth/findwellness
- Online Therapy for Trauma Help-Remote Counseling For Grief
    - www.hopeforthejourney.org/ptsd/trauma
- Houston Child Therapy
    - www.joanlipisek.com

These are just a few, please choose the appropriate assistance that fits your family's needs.

Big Mama and PaPa 50th Wedding Anniversary.

CPSIA information can be obtained
at www.ICGtesting.com
Printed in the USA
LVHW072254141021
700493LV00002B/4